Scary Show

A. B. Saddlewick

BUSTER

Chapter One

Maud had never seen the monsters of Rotwood so excited. A large crowd bustled around the entrance of the school, and other pupils were running over to join them. As Maud approached, she heard gasps, roars and growls. What was going on? Had one of the gargoyles fallen from the roof and hurt itself?

Maud pushed her way through. Danny the demon's wings were beating rapidly, and she had to leap aside to avoid them. At last she reached the front.

Pinned to the school noticeboard, just above

the poster for the lunchtime Spell Club, was a scrap of parchment with large, spidery writing:

SPECIAL ANNOUNCEMENT

ROTWOOD'S GOT TALENT

Will you make the crowd SCREAM with delight?
Can you cast a SPELL over an audience?
Do you have the HEX FACTOR?

SHOW US ALL YOUR MOST
MONSTROUS SKILLS IN THIS YEAR'S
END-OF-TERM TALENT SHOW!

Please note: the talent show is compulsory.
No exceptions.

Maud spotted her friends Wilf and Paprika on the other side of the crowd and pushed her way over to them. Wilf's wolf-tail was wagging, and Paprika was grinning so widely she could see his vampire fangs.

"I'm going to show off my agility skills," said Wilf.

"I'm doing some synchronised flying with the other vampires," said Paprika.

"I'm going to try my gymnastics routine again," said a voice next to them. It had to belong to Invisible Isabel.

"What are you going to do, Maud?" asked Paprika.

Maud felt her cheeks flushing. What could she possibly do to entertain an audience of monsters? Everyone else would be showing off their monster powers, but she didn't have any. She was just a human.

"I'm going to … er …"

"Yeah, what exactly can you do?" said a voice from behind.

Maud turned around and saw Poisonous

Penelope peering at her. The witch's hands were planted on her hips, and there was a smirk on her pale green face.

Maud wished she'd never pretended to be a monster called a 'Tutu'. Penelope was always questioning her about it. But she wouldn't have been allowed to stay at a monster school if she'd admitted she was human.

"Well … er …" said Maud.

The school bell tolled just in time. Maud breathed a sigh of relief, as the pupils began to file up the stone steps. She'd been spared humiliation for now, but the end of term was just a week away. She needed to come up with something fast.

Maud plodded across the gloomy entrance hall. All around her, she could hear monsters discussing the contest. A group of ogres from the year above were planning a weightlifting display. A bunch of hairy trolls from the year below were forming a heavy-metal band.

Maud's pet rat Quentin poked his head out of her pocket, his snout quivering.

"How can I possibly impress this lot?" she asked him. "Should we revive our magic act?"

Quentin squeaked with fear and ducked back into Maud's pocket. At the talent contest in her old school, Maud had tried to saw Quentin in half. Unfortunately, he'd had an attack of stage fright and run away, so she'd had to use her packed lunch for the trick instead. Even the teachers hadn't bothered to applaud.

Maud walked down the long corridor at the back of the hall to the Rotwood science lab for her first lesson. She took a stool between Paprika and Oscar, who was detaching his head.

"I'm going to do my ventriloquist act," said Oscar. He placed his head in his lap. "Good evening, boys and girls!" it said.

"I don't think that counts," said Paprika. "You're supposed to throw your voice, not your whole head."

Professor Gool walked in. He had dark shadows under his eyes and grey skin, but that was how he normally looked. He took a key out of his lab-coat pocket.

"Settle down, monsters," he shouted, the white tufts of hair on either side of his head wiggling up and down. "I know you're excited about the contest, but you're here to learn, not to show off."

The murmur in the room died down, and Oscar stuck his head back on.

"Today we'll be examining dangerous spiders," said Professor Gool.

He unlocked the cupboard under his desk and heaved out a large plastic tank. Reaching inside, he lifted up a black spider with four red eyes, too many legs and a flicking tail.

"This is the highly monstrous scorpion spider," said Professor Gool. "One sting contains enough venom to kill a human in less than a second."

The spider scuttled up Professor Gool's arm, and the class cooed.

"Cute!" said Invisible Isabel.

"I'm going to pass him around, so be very careful," said Professor Gool. "He's a fragile little creature. I don't want him coming back with only thirteen legs."

He handed the spider over to the monsters at the front table, who crowded round to pet it.

This was just the sort of lesson Maud usually loved, but all she could think about was the contest.

Paprika nudged her. "What's up?"

"It's the show," whispered Maud. "I don't know what I'm going to do. I'm not a monster, remember?" Paprika was the one monster in all of Rotwood who knew Maud's secret. Unless you counted Mr Von Bat, Paprika's dad and Maud's class teacher.

Professor Gool pointed at Maud. "Montague!" he shouted. His cheeks were red, and the tufts of hair on his head were sticking up. "Name the three most terrifying spiders in order of monstrosity."

"Yes, Sir," said Maud. "Number three is the poison-spitting yellow huntsman. Number two is the red-horned nostril-burrower. And number one is the Australian toilet-seat-lurker."

Professor Gool looked a little disappointed, the tufts of hair sinking down again. "Correct, but it still doesn't give you the right to jabber away willy-nilly."

After the lesson, Maud followed the other pupils out into the playground, among the wonky, weather-beaten gravestones.

A skeleton pupil called Billy Bones ran up to her. "We're playing Monsterball, Maud. Wanna join us?"

"No, thanks," said Maud.

She sat down on a patch of overgrown grass, leaned against a mossy headstone and watched as Billy and Oscar picked teams. Paprika and Zombie Zak were last to be chosen. Billy scratched his bare skull for a moment and pointed at Paprika.

"Monstrous!" shouted Paprika. "I wasn't last!"

"Ug!" shouted Zak, shuffling over to Oscar's team.

Oscar whipped his head off his shoulders and threw it up in the air to begin the game. It grinned as it spun round and round in the air. Maud wished she could rip her head off and fling it around like that. But if you tore a human head off, it wasn't so easy to put it back again.

She stared gloomily at the crumbling graves. At her old school, Primrose Towers, she'd felt like the odd one out because she hated pink dresses and fluffy bunnies. Now she was the odd one out because she had no special powers. Maybe she'd never fit in anywhere.

Something thudded in front of her.

"Hi Maud," it said.

Maud peered into the long grass. Oscar's head spat out a clump of grass and smiled muddily.

Billy Bones was rushing over, Oscar's body following, feeling the way with its hands and stumbling into gravestones.

"It's over here!" shouted Maud. She grabbed Oscar's hair and lifted his head up.

There was a sudden rustle from the trees at the edge of the graveyard. Maud heard a voice.

"This can't be the way," it said. "You're looking at the map wrong. As usual."

"We're on the right trail, dear," replied another voice. "It's just a little overgrown."

An elderly man and woman stumbled out into the yard.

Humans! What were they doing in Rotwood Forest?

The elderly couple were wearing waterproof jackets, hiking boots and rucksacks with pans, torches and can-openers hanging from metal frames. The man was holding a map.

The old man smiled at Maud and was just about to speak when he saw Oscar's head. His mouth stayed open, and he dropped the map.

"Hey!" shouted Oscar's head. "This is private property!"

The couple looked at each other, screamed, then turned and ran into the forest, their pots and pans clanking.

Oscar's head shook in Maud's hand, as he sniggered.

A few graves along, Billy Bones was doubled up with laughter. "Humans, eh?"

"I know," said Maud, forcing a smile. "Stupid, stupid humans."

Chapter Two

The Head of History, Dr Reaper, peered out from the hood of his thick, black cloak, his withered lips drawn tightly over his sharp teeth.

"The lassst of the troll armiesss fell at the battle of Ossslo," he hissed. "The Vikingsss had banisssshed them to the desssolate, icy North, where they ressside today."

The bell rang, and everyone in the classroom started to shuffle about.

Dr Reaper pointed a bony finger at them, as they gathered their things. "You'll want to remember all of that for your tesssts."

Maud packed her pencil case and made her way out. She passed an alcove lit by a dripping candle, and spotted Penelope muttering to Wilf's brother Warren.

"It will be so much fun to watch a proper talent show," said Penelope. "I saw one of those human ones on TV once. There was a magician, a dancing dog and a woman singing show-tunes who was even hairier than you."

"Pathetic," growled Warren.

"I know," said Penelope. She spotted Maud and added, "Humans are so one-dimensional."

Maud cringed and strode past with her head down. *I need a talent,* she thought, *and I think I might know where to find one.* She took the stairs to the library.

When she opened the door, dust swirled around her. High windows threw thin shafts of light on to hundreds of leather-bound books. They'd been stuffed on to the shelves every which way.

Mr Shakespeare, the school librarian, was sitting behind the desk at the far side of the room, dipping a feather into a pot of ink. He was wearing his doublet and hose and a white shirt with a wide collar.

"How dost thou, Maud?" he asked.

"I'm fine, thank you," said Maud. "I'm not interrupting, am I? I don't want to disrupt one of your brilliant plays."

"Plays?" asked Mr Shakespeare. "Alas, no. My agent has told me to concentrate on movies. I'm working on *Hamlet Cop*, *Macbeth v. Predator* and *Romeo and Juliet and Ninjas*."

"They sound … er … interesting," said Maud. She glanced around the shelves, but all she could see were cracked leather spines and crumbling bindings. She wasn't sure Mr Shakespeare used the Dewey decimal system.

"Do you have anything that might help me develop a talent?" asked Maud. "The sort I could impress a crowd with."

Mr Shakespeare leaned forward. A candle on his desk lit up his face eerily. "You seek the concealed arts that confound the ignorant and amaze the very faculties of eyes and ears?" he asked.

"I suppose so," said Maud.

"You'll be wanting the hobbies section, then," he said.

He led her over to a lopsided shelf and moved aside a stack of ancient books with yellow pages. Underneath was a pile of modern paperbacks with titles like *Card Tricks for Beginners*, *Maximise Your Memory*, *Ventriloquism for Dummies*, *Plate-Spinning Basics* and *Juggling – An Amateur's Guide*.

"Monstrous!" said Maud, scooping up the books. "I'll bring them back next week."

"As you like it," said Mr Shakespeare.

Maud left the library feeling better than she had all day. The pile of books was so tall that she couldn't see over the top, and she had to be careful not to squash Quentin. "I'll have a talent in no time," she muttered. "I'll show ..." *Thud!*

Maud crashed straight into someone. The books went flying from her hands. Penelope was sprawled on the floor and scowling. Her bag had fallen open, and jars of newt eyes, frog toes and dog tongues were rolling down the corridor.

"I don't know what you're planning for the talent show," said Penelope, getting to her feet again, "but I hope it isn't a balancing act."

"Sorry," said Maud. She knelt and gathered her books.

Penelope glanced at them and narrowed her eyes. "Card tricks? Plate-spinning? Juggling?" she snorted. "Aren't you going to give us a display of your Tutu powers?"

"Of course," said Maud. "I ... er ... thought

I'd warm up with something different. Get some variety into the act."

Penelope grinned. "I can't wait to see what you come up with. It's going to be the highlight of my night."

She muttered and waggled her fingers. The jars rolled back along the floor and flew into her bag, which floated up into her arms.

"Monstrous," said Maud. "Could you do that with my books?"

Penelope smiled. "Of course I *could*," she said. "But I'm not going to." She cackled and sauntered off.

Chapter Three

Maud balanced the china plate on the end of the broom. She pushed the edge, and the plate spun once, twice … then toppled off. SMASH! The plate splintered into hundreds of tiny pieces on the garage floor.

"Drat," said Maud, slumping on to her dad's work-bench. She looked at the mess around her. The bits of plate had joined several bent playing cards she'd tried to shove up her sleeve and a trio of squashed oranges she'd tried to juggle.

Quentin was sitting in the middle of the mess, nibbling the Ace of Hearts.

"It's all a lot harder than it looks, isn't it, Quent?" asked Maud.

Quentin sniffed at the splattered oranges and nodded.

High parps echoed from the living room. Maud's twin sister Milly had been practising her clarinet solo for the Primrose Towers School Concert all evening. She sounded like a flock of angry ducks.

Quentin squeaked and buried his head under a pile of cards.

"I know," said Maud. "Let's just try and block it out."

Maud looked around for *Maximise Your Memory*. It wasn't in the pile of books next to her bag. It wasn't underneath the stack of plates she'd brought in from the kitchen. And it wasn't underneath the scattered playing cards.

So much for amazing feats of memory. She couldn't even remember where she'd put the book.

"Why would the Rotwood monsters even care about these stupid party tricks anyway?" she said, running her finger down the spines of the books. "So what if I can spin plates or juggle or remember things or ..."

She stopped on an ancient black book with a battered spine. She peered closer. In faded gold lettering it said: *Advanced Sorcery: Volume One.* That was odd. She couldn't remember seeing that in the books Mr Shakespeare had given her.

Maud grabbed the book and opened the cover. *Please return to Penelope Prenderghast, Class 3B, Rotwood School,* she read. *Or else.*

Maud turned the page. There was a large red triangle and the words, *These spells are to be attempted by trained witches and wizards only. Hey Presto Press accepts no responsibility for any foolish amateurs who gaze upon its forbidden contents.*

"Look at this!" said Maud.

Quentin glanced up from his gnawed playing card.

"Penelope must have missed this when she magicked everything back into her bag,'" said Maud. "I suppose I'd better give it back to her first thing on Monday."

She hesitated. "It wouldn't be right for me to read it after that fearsome warning," she said. "Would it?"

Quentin went back to chewing the card.

"You're right," said Maud. "A little peek wouldn't hurt."

Quentin squeaked and shook his head, but Maud ignored him. She flicked through the pages. There was a spell to make you fly, a spell that let you read minds and one that allowed you to shift into the form of over seventy different animals. But all the spells needed strange ingredients like dragon scales, basilisk teeth and unicorn tails. She was pretty sure her mum didn't have any of those in the pantry.

"Yep, this is pretty advanced stuff," she said. "Never mind."

Maud was about to shut the book when she spotted something in the 'Potions' section.

For the Breathing of Fire
By Venomous Veronica

YOU WILL NEED:
One cup of vinegar
Two tablespoons of mustard
Half a red pepper
Three mushrooms
A sprinkle of magic

METHOD
Combine the ingredients in a cauldron or pan
and leave in the moonlight.

Maud was pretty sure they had all that stuff in the house. Well, everything except the magic, and it was worth a try, surely. The instructions sounded incredibly simple. All she had to do was mix them in a pan, and soon she could be blowing out massive flames.

"No!" said Maud. She closed the book and tossed it aside. The warning had said only trained sorcerers could perform the spells.

Maud turned to the juggling book instead.

"Imagine if I did four balls at once," she said. "Everyone at Rotwood would love that, wouldn't they?"

Quentin squinted at her, then went back to chewing the Ace of Hearts.

It was no use. All Maud could think about was how utterly monstrous it would be if she stood in front of everyone and snorted fire out of her nostrils. As the audience got to its feet and cheered, she'd look over at Penelope, stick her tongue out, and breathe a long flame just for her.

Maud rushed into the kitchen, pulled open the fridge and sifted through the vegetable drawer. Tucked at the back, behind an iceberg lettuce and a punnet of strawberries, were three mushrooms and half a pepper.

"Monstrous!" said Maud.

"What's monstrous?"

Maud slammed the tray shut and spun around. Her sister Milly was peering at her.

"Those vegetables," said Maud.

"You don't usually get excited about vegetables," said Milly. "Remember that time Dad said you couldn't have any chocolate snaps until you'd finished your broccoli?"

"It's for school," said Maud. "We've got to grow a mould culture on a mushroom for Science class."

"The last thing you need in that place is more mould," said Milly, twirling over to the sink and making herself a glass of squash. "Can't you just scrape some off the walls?"

"Actually, Mr Quasimodo keeps the place very clean," said Maud. "He even changed the water in his bucket last week."

"It would take more than a bucket of water to make that place acceptable," said Milly. "You'd need a million cans of air freshener at least."

Milly glugged her squash and plonked the glass on the side.

"Better get back to it," she said, walking out again. "Mum and Dad spent a fortune on my lovely clarinet, and I don't want to let them down by only coming second in the concert."

Maud grabbed the mushrooms, mustard, vinegar and pepper and took them out into the garage. She took a rusty copper pan down from one of the high shelves and mixed everything together with one of her dad's spanners. Then, holding her empty hands over the pan, she tried waggling them the way she'd seen Penelope do.

Nothing happened. A mushroom stem and a piece of pepper rose to the top, and Maud pushed them down again. The mixture looked more like school-dinner leftovers than a magic potion, but she guessed it would be different once the moonlight and the spell did their work.

Maud stuck the pan underneath the garage windows and flung them open. She could already see the moon rising, and there were no clouds in the dusky sky. Perfect.

An acidic smell was wafting from the pan. Quentin winced, as Maud lifted him into his cage next to it.

"Sorry about the pong," said Maud. "It'll be worth it when I'm snorting fire in the school hall."

Maud switched off the light and headed up to bed. For the first time, she was actually looking forward to the talent contest.

Chapter Four

The next morning, Maud squinted at her alarm clock. It was five to seven. She threw her covers aside and leapt out of bed.

Maud tiptoed through the mess on her side of the room she shared with her sister. She stepped into the murky hallway and gasped. A strange creature was approaching. Its head was wrapped like a mummy, its skin was green and glowing, and its eyes were dark, empty sockets. Maud's pulse quickened as she backed away. She wondered if the hideous imp had been sent to punish her for meddling in the black arts.

The monster raised a hand and flicked the light switch.

"Get out of my way," it said.

Maud let out a sigh of relief. It was just Milly, with a towel wrapped around her head and a green moisturising mask over her whole face apart from her eyes. She pushed past into the bedroom.

Maud scrambled down the stairs, jumping the last two and landing with a thud on the hallway floor. She darted over to the door at the side of the kitchen, opened it, and switched on the garage light.

The mixture had risen high overnight. There was a stain running down the side of the pan where it had overflowed. Maud saw that the pepper and mushroom had dissolved completely, leaving a gloopy brown liquid with large bubbles on top.

Quentin was resting on his haunches, with his paws on his stomach.

"Poor Quentin," said Maud, crouching down. She noticed a bit of the gloop had trickled into his cage. "The smell of that liquid didn't make you feel ill, did it?"

Quentin's eyes widened for a moment, and he let out a loud burp. A ball of fire shot out of his mouth and flew across the garage.

Maud ducked aside as the flame exploded on the far wall, leaving a round black scorch mark. The spell had worked! Some of the magic at Rotwood must have rubbed off on Maud.

"Oh no," said Maud. "What have you done?"

Quentin looked down at the puddle of liquid, then up at Maud.

"You ate it?" said Maud. "That wasn't supposed to be for you, Quent!"

She unscrewed his water bottle from the side of his cage. "Hold your breath a minute."

She rushed into the kitchen. Her dad was sitting at the table reading *Exhaust Pipe Enthusiast* magazine. He glanced at her and shoved his large glasses up the bridge of his nose. "Can you smell burning, dear?"

"That was me," said Maud. "I overdid the toast earlier on."

"Well, that's what you get for messing with the dial," said her dad, looking back at his magazine.

Maud filled the bottle up and hurried back into the garage. She closed the door and tiptoed over to Quentin's cage.

His stomach rumbled loudly, and his cheeks puffed up.

"Try and hold it in," said Maud. She fixed Quentin's bottle to his cage. He stood up on his hind legs and drank from the nozzle, his whiskers twitching back and forth as he gulped.

"Get as much down as you can," said Maud.

Quentin drank until all the water was gone. Tiny plumes of smoke wafted out of his ears.

"Any better?" Maud asked.

Quentin squeaked. WHOOMPH! Another fireball shot across the room and scorched the wooden thermometer on the wall. The mercury shot up the glass and exploded from the top.

"Oh dear," said Maud. "You'd better try and keep quiet from now on."

Quentin squeaked agreement. This time he chirped out a flame that melted his running wheel into a splodge of plastic.

"Hmm," said Maud. "This isn't working."

She looked around the shelves for something she could use as a muzzle. There was a roll of wire and a clothes peg, but she didn't think either would be very comfortable. Then she saw a small, red rubber band. She doubled it up and looped it over Quentin's jaw.

"Not too tight?" asked Maud.

Quentin shook his head.

Maud grabbed the ancient magic book from the floor and turned to the index at the back.

She ran her finger down the uneven page until she found:

REVERSAL – full details of how to reverse the spells in this book can be found in *Advanced Sorcery: Volume Two.*

Well, that's just perfect, thought Maud.

She picked Quentin up and dropped him into her pocket, casting a glance at the gloopy liquid in the pan. The book had been right. The potion did make you breathe fire – every time you opened your mouth. If she tried sipping some before the talent show, she'd burn down the entire school and the surrounding forest, too.

It looked as if she was back to square one.

Except now she had a flame-throwing rat to deal with, too.

Chapter Five

Maud spread marmalade on her toast and took a bite. Quentin peered up hopefully from inside her pocket.

"Sorry, Quent," she whispered. "I can't give you any today. We'd all be toast if I took that muzzle off."

Milly slurped her porridge, humming her clarinet solo. "What are all those books you've been lugging around?" she asked. "I found one about memory tricks under the sofa last night. You're such a weirdo."

"We're having a talent contest," said Maud.

"Which is a problem for me because I don't have any."

Maud's mum glanced up from her paper and peered over the top of her large, round glasses.

"Don't say that, dear," she said. "You've got plenty of talents."

"Like what?" asked Maud.

"Well …" Mrs Montague stared at her for a second. "You're good at collecting worms. You dug up a whole jar of them that time we helped Auntie Agnes out with her vegetable patch."

"Don't remind me of that," scowled Milly. "She left it under our bed, and I was finding the horrible slimy things under my pillow for weeks afterwards."

"It wasn't my fault the lid came off," said Maud. "Anyway, it doesn't matter. That's not the sort of skill you can show off on stage."

She slumped forward on to the table with her head in her hands. "This is going to be a disaster!"

Milly placed her hand on her shoulder. "I know it must seem unfair that you don't have any talents, while I have so many. Believe me, if I could give you one of mine, I would."

"Maybe you could teach Maud something," said Mrs Montague. "How about one of your dance routines?"

"Oh Mum," moaned Milly. "Do I have to?"

"Well, dear," said Mrs Montague, "a moment ago you were saying you wanted to help Maud out, remember?"

Milly took a mouthful of porridge and glared at Maud. "Alright. It's not going to be easy though."

Maud climbed down from the bus and tramped across the gravel to Rotwood. She looked over at the poster for the talent show, hoping that it would have a big 'cancelled' banner slapped across it. No such luck.

A hand tapped Maud on the shoulder. She turned around and saw her class teacher, Mr Von Bat, wearing his swishing black cape.

"We've been talking about you in the staff crypt," he said. "And it hasn't been positive."

"Oh?" asked Maud. She wondered what she was in trouble for now. Nothing seemed to be going her way at the moment.

"Professor Gool and Dr Reaper both said you were very distracted in your lessons," said Mr Von Bat. "I thought I'd better talk to you about it out here in case it was something to do with your ..." He looked over his shoulder and dropped his voice to a whisper, "... condition."

Maud nodded. Mr Von Bat had been keeping quiet about the fact that she was a human, and in return she'd agreed not to tell anyone that he was secretly a human, too.

"It's this talent show," said Maud. "Everyone else has got amazing powers to show off, and

I've got nothing."

"Powers don't matter," replied the teacher. "Just be yourself."

Mr Von Bat rearranged his fake plastic fangs.

"Be myself?" asked Maud. She could feel her shoulders knotting up. "Be myself? You spend all day pretending to be a vampire when the truth is you're as human as me and you've got about as much chance of turning into a bat as I have of turning into a motorbike."

"Alright," said Mr Von Bat. "I was only trying to help."

"If you really want to help, cancel the talent show," said Maud.

"I'm afraid that won't be possible," said Mr Von Bat. He pointed to the steps outside the entrance, where Billy Bones was playing the spoons on his ribs for Oscar. "As you can see, the event has caught the imagination of the whole school. Do you think we should call it off just to make you feel more comfortable?"

Maud looked over at Billy. He finished by clattering the spoon on his skull, and threw his hands out to the sides. Oscar clapped. The pair of them looked like they were having the time of their lives.

"I suppose not," she said.

"Right," said Mr Von Bat. "Well, stop mooning around and prepare for the show." He straightened out his cape and strode off towards the school.

Maud followed, dragging her shoes on the gravel.

Chapter Six

Paprika met up with Maud at lunchtime. "You look frazzled," he said.

Maud felt the back of her hair. Had Quentin singed it with one of his fiery burps? It didn't feel any different.

"What do you mean 'frizzled'?" she asked.

"Not 'frizzled'," laughed Paprika, "'frazzled'! I mean you look tired."

"Oh," said Maud, "I am." She looked across the school cafeteria. Everyone looked so excited and happy as they queued for the food cauldrons and sat on the rickety benches. "I've had a bit of trouble with Quentin this morning."

Maud lifted her pet rat out of her pocket and on to the table. He pulled at his rubber-band muzzle with his paws, but it twanged in his face and made him somersault backwards.

"I think he wants to take that off," said Paprika. He gently lifted the tiny muzzle over Quentin's head.

Quentin let out a flaming blue burp that made him look like a Bunsen burner. It blasted on to Paprika's bowl of frogspawn custard, glazing the top.

"On second thoughts," said Paprika, "he should probably keep it on."

He lowered the muzzle back down over Quentin's nose. "What a mean spell to cast," he said. "Was it Penelope?"

"It was me, actually," said Maud. "By mistake."

Maud looked down at her bowl of newts' legs. She'd grown fond of them since she started at Rotwood, but she didn't feel hungry today.

"I mixed a potion from one of Penelope's books," said Maud. "I meant to drink it myself, but poor Quentin got to it first. I know it was dangerous, but I'm desperate for a skill to show off in the talent contest."

"There must be something you can do," said Paprika.

"I can't think of anything," said Maud, pushing a floppy brown newt's leg around the edge of her bowl. "And I'm running out of time." Maud lifted Quentin back into her pocket and stood up. "But I'll keep trying."

"Good luck," said Paprika. "I'm sure you'll manage it."

Maud took her bowl over to the large green toad at the back of the hall and scraped her leftovers into its mouth. It swallowed them and croaked appreciatively.

Maud trudged back to the staircase and made her way to the library.

Mr Shakespeare was sitting behind his desk,

scribbling frantically. He glanced at her and said, "Well met, good Maud."

"Is your screenplay going well?" asked Maud.

"Excellently," said Mr Shakespeare. He lifted up his quill and cleared his throat. "Is this an automatic assault rifle I see before me, the handle toward my hand? Yes, it is. Eat lead!"

Mr Shakespeare made a gun noise out of the side of his mouth and looked at Maud, expectantly.

"Er … monstrous," she said. "But I need you to find a book for me. It's called *Advanced Sorcery: Volume Two*. Do you know where it is?"

"I fear I checked that one out recently," said Mr Shakespeare. He shoved his scroll aside and opened a notebook. "Yes, it went to a wart-nosed little malcontent named Penelope Prenderghast."

"Drat!" said Maud. There was no way Penelope would let her look up the reversal spell. "Oh well. Thanks anyway."

"Fare thee well," said Mr Shakespeare. He picked up his quill and dipped it in his inkpot. "Now for the car chase."

Later that evening, Maud was lying on her bed and flipping through Penelope's spell book. She'd meant to give it back, but she was so desperate to find a skill for the contest she couldn't resist another look.

Quentin was lying next to her on the bunk, snoozing. He'd finally stopped trying to claw his muzzle off.

Maud glanced over at Milly's dolls, which were arranged in a neat row on top of her dressing table.

"This will cheer you up," said Maud. "It's called the 'Telekinesis Spell'. It makes things float into the air when I point and click my fingers."

Quentin leapt behind the pillow and trembled so hard he made it shake.

"Don't worry, I won't point at you," said Maud. "I'll make Milly's Pink Pony Princess Party Dolls float up and have a sky battle. You'd like that, wouldn't you?"

Quentin stuck his muzzle over the edge of the pillow. Maud held her hand up and read from the book.

Telekinesis Spell
By Spiteful Sally, aged 126

Blast away into the sky,
Fast, fast, rise up high,
Swift as breeze, light as air,
Drift around without a care!

Maud put the book down on the bed, clicked her fingers and pointed at Bethany Blossom. She stared at the plastic pony with its huge blue eyes and glittery mane, waiting for it to rise. Nothing happened.

Maud's stomach felt funny. She looked down and saw her feet leaving the carpet. She flapped her arms, but it didn't stop her body drifting up.

"Uh-oh!" shouted Maud. "That's not meant to happen."

She tried to dive down, but it felt as if the room was full of treacle. Her head bobbed up until it brushed the lampshade. Quentin looked up from the lower bunk, whiskers trembling.

Maud felt her legs drift up until they were touching the ceiling. She reached down and managed to grasp the frame of the bunk bed. She pulled herself over to it and tried to drag herself down, but it was no use. Whenever she tried to force herself down, she popped right back up again.

With a huge effort, Maud looped her hands and feet around the metal frame of the top bunk and held herself down against the mattress.

The door thwacked open, and Milly looked up at her.

"What are you doing on my bed?" she said.

"I'm … er … looking for Quentin," said Maud. "I think he crawled up here."

Milly shrieked and ran out of the door.

As her body hovered back up, Maud could hear Milly stomping downstairs. "Muuuum!" screamed her sister. "Hideous vermin is in my bed again!"

Maud heard her mum's muffled voice saying, "That's no way to talk about your sister."

"I don't mean her," shouted Milly. "I mean her mangy pet rat."

Maud heard footsteps coming along the hallway. She pushed off from the bed and kicked against the ceiling, desperately trying to force herself down to the floor. But she floated right back up like a bobbing balloon.

She could hear her mum coming up the stairs. How on earth was she going to explain this?

Maud tried to remember the instructions in the spell book. All they'd said was that you had to read the words out and click your fingers.

She tried clicking her fingers again.

Maud flopped down to the floor with a horrible crunch. She lay still for a moment, waiting for her breath to come back. She stood up and felt her arms. Neither of them seemed to be broken.

Maud looked down and gasped. "Oh no!" On the floor was a mangled mess that had once been a clarinet.

Chapter Seven

Maud picked up the pieces of the clarinet. The metal valves were bent and twisted. This wasn't something she could fix with a bit of glue.

Milly flung the door open and let out a screech. Mrs Montague followed her into the room.

"I'm sorry," said Maud. "I …"

"What on earth have you done, Maud?" asked Mrs Montague, grabbing the broken pieces. "I'm very disappointed in you."

"It was an accident," said Maud.

Over by the door, Milly was still screeching.

Mrs Montague examined the pieces. "We'll have to see what the man in the shop says. But I doubt he'll be able to fix it in time for the concert."

Milly's scream rose in pitch.

"I'm sorry," said Maud. "I really didn't mean to do it. I'll do anything to make it up to you."

Milly cut off mid-scream. Her eyes were streaming. "Anything?" she asked.

"Yes," said Maud.

"Okay," said Milly. "Let me think about it."

Maud thought she saw a sly grin flit across Milly's face as she dabbed her eyes.

Mrs Montague took Milly's hand and led her downstairs, casting one last disapproving glance behind her. Maud sat down on the bed. She tried to think about all the times her sister had been horrible to her, but it was no use. She still felt guilty.

A short while later, the doorbell rang. Maud was still sitting on the bed.

"Maud, your friend's here!" shouted her dad.

Maud couldn't remember inviting any of her friends. Wilf and Paprika certainly hadn't mentioned anything about popping round.

"Go right up," said Mr Montague. "She's in her room."

Maud heard feet stomping up the stairs. Her door was flung open to reveal Poisonous Penelope. She pointed a warty finger at Maud.

"I know you've got it," she said. "Give it back."

"Give what back?" asked Maud.

Penelope looked around the room.

"That!" she said, pointing to the open spell book on the bed. "I knew you were the thief."

"Sorry," said Maud, closing the book and offering it to Penelope. "I wasn't trying to steal it. It just got jumbled in with my stuff."

Penelope snatched the book and examined it. "At least you haven't damaged it."

"I was going to give it back to you first thing tomorrow," said Maud. "In fact, I needed to speak to you about something, seeing as how you're the best in our school at magic."

Penelope tucked the book under her arm and peered at Maud. "What is it?"

"I wondered if you could give me a reversal spell for this," said Maud.

She lifted Quentin out of her pocket and pulled his muzzle down, long enough for him to squeak out a fireball that flew over to the wall and burned a hole in her 'Maggots of the World' wall chart. Maud whipped the muzzle back up again.

"A reversal spell?" snorted Penelope. "There's no such thing as a reversal spell for a potion. Everyone knows that. You just have to leave it to run its course."

"And how long will that be?" asked Maud.

"Oh, not long," said Penelope. "A couple of years."

Quentin looked up at Maud and gulped.

"A couple of years?" said Maud.

"At least," muttered Penelope. She flipped through the spell book. "What else have you been using this for?"

"I tried the telekinesis spell," said Maud. "But it didn't work very well. It made me float up in the air instead of the things I pointed at."

Penelope let out a loud cackle. "Don't tell me you read it forwards. What sort of idiot doesn't know that some spells are meant to be read backwards?"

"Ah yes, I remember now," said Maud. "It must have slipped my mind."

"Here's how it's done," said Penelope. She closed the book and recited:

Care a without around drift,
Air as light, breeze as swift,
High up rise, fast, fast,
Sky the into away blast.

Penelope snapped her fingers and pointed at Quentin. He started to rise above the bed. He glanced to one side and then the other, with his paws scrabbling around helplessly.

"Let him go!" said Maud, leaping up from the bed.

Penelope drew her hand back, and Quentin shot across the room.

"It's Super Rat," shouted Penelope, twisting her arm so Quentin swerved from side to side. "Ta-dah!"

She held her hand still, and Quentin hovered over Milly's fish tank. He looked down at the water with his fur standing on end.

"Stop it," said Maud. "He isn't enjoying it."

"Fine," said Penelope. "Looks like the Tutu can't take a joke."

She lowered her hand until Quentin was safely on the floor. He scuttled across the room and crawled inside a dirty sock under the bed.

Penelope turned to Maud and narrowed her

eyes. "There are a lot of things Tutus can't do, aren't there? Like perform magic."

"We just have a different sort of magic," said Maud. "We can ... er ... jump back in time just by sneezing."

"Go on then," said Penelope.

Maud closed her eyes and faked a sneeze.

She opened them again and wiped her hand across her forehead. "Phew! Just went back to Ancient Rome. It was pretty monstrous."

"Hmm," said Penelope. She walked over to the window and looked outside. "So what do I know about you so-called 'Tutus'? Well, you live in semi-detached houses, drive cars and shop in supermarkets, just like humans. You've got no special powers, just like humans. And you look and sound just like humans."

"Yes, I've never really thought of it like that before," said Maud. She opened the door. "I expect you'll want to be getting back now."

Penelope clicked her fingers and pointed at

the door. It slammed shut.

"Admit it," she said. "There's no such thing as a Tutu."

"Of course there is," said Maud. She tried to laugh, but all that came out was a nervous giggle. "Anyway, I need to get on with my homework now, so let's catch up tomorrow."

"I'm not going anywhere until you admit you're human," said Penelope.

Maud tried desperately to think of reasons why her family just *seemed* human. But what would be the point? Penelope knew the truth. She couldn't deny it any more.

Maud slumped down on to her bunk. "Okay. I admit it."

"Ha!" said Penelope. "I knew it!"

Maud looked up at Penelope. "You won't tell anyone, will you?"

"Why shouldn't I?"

Maud pointed to Milly's collection of Pink Princess Pony Party Dolls.

"That pony is called Bethany Blossom," said Maud. "That one's called Rihanna Rainbow. And that's Saffron Sparkle."

Penelope looked over at the dolls. "That's horrible. Why are you telling me this?"

"Because the girls in my old school love those ponies," said Maud. "They talk about them all the time. And they love flower-arranging and baking cupcakes and drawing pictures of fluffy kittens."

The cuteness overload was making Penelope tremble. A bead of sweat was running down her cheek.

"If you tell everyone I'm human, I'll get sent back to that school," said Maud. "Would you really wish that on me?"

Penelope turned back to Maud. "It's not my problem. But I don't need to tell people anyway.

As soon as the talent show comes around, everyone in the school will be able to see how ordinary you are with their own two eyes. Or with their own one eye, in the case of Simon the cyclops."

Penelope left with a smirk on her face. Maud swung her legs on to the bed and lay back, looking up at the top bunk. Penelope was right. She was just a couple of days away from being found out, and no amount of cramming could stop the inevitable.

"Face it, Maud," she muttered. "Your Rotwood days are numbered."

Chapter Eight

$\mathcal{M}$illy was smiling. "Heard the good news?" she asked at breakfast.

Maud sat down and rubbed her eyes. She'd woken up dozens of times in the night worrying about what Penelope had said, and she was exhausted.

"The shop can mend my clarinet in time," said Milly. "It wasn't so bad after all."

Maud dipped a knife into the marmalade jar and scraped it over a piece of toast. "I thought your concert was tonight," she said.

"It is," said Milly. She scooped up a spoonful

of porridge and blew on it. "That's why I've decided to enter your talent contest instead."

Maud choked on her toast.

"I know," said Milly. "Isn't it fab? I'm sure to wipe the floor with those Rotwood rejects."

Maud took a sip of orange juice to dislodge the chunk of toast in her throat. "You can't enter a talent contest at someone else's school," she said. "It's against the rules."

"That's funny," said Milly, "because I remember you saying you'd do anything to make it up to me. Maybe I was imagining it."

"No," said Maud. "But I didn't mean it like that."

Mrs Montague flicked her newspaper down and tutted at Maud. "You did say you'd do anything, dear."

"There must be something else I can do," said Maud.

"It's too late to go back on your word now," said Milly.

"I know," said Maud. "But it wouldn't be fair on the others if you turned up and won the contest."

Milly shrugged and grinned.

Maud trooped upstairs. Now she'd have to try and convince everyone that her sister was a monster, too. Maybe if Milly had one of her tantrums, they'd assume she was a bad-tempered banshee.

She grabbed her rucksack off the bed, but as she did so a yellowing sheet of paper fluttered out from underneath. She picked it up and unfolded it. It was a spell written in neat calligraphy. It must have fallen out of Penelope's book. But what did it do? There was no title or instructions.

Maud stared at the spell, biting her lip. She could ask Penelope about it … but it wasn't as though the witch would tell her the truth.

The spell read:

Brothers and sisters, skulls and bones,
Others' power for your own,
Touch or brush, steal or pinch,
Clutch or tap, it's a cinch.

The words didn't make a lot of sense to Maud. After all the trouble of the fire-breathing potion, Maud knew she should rip up the spell and throw it in the bin. But she couldn't stop herself staring at it. What if it gave her a brilliant talent that would let her win the contest?

Maud decided it was worth the risk. She read the spell out loud, remembering to start at the end this time. She looked down at the floor. It didn't seem to be sinking. She clicked her fingers and pointed at the Bethany Blossom doll. Nothing happened. Maud shrugged. She was sure she'd read it right. Maybe it only worked in certain places or at certain times, or you needed a potion to go with it. Oh well.

Milly stomped in and shoved past Maud. She switched on her CD-player and immediately it began to blast out the 'Pink Princess Pony Party Friendship Song'.

"Not now, Milly, please," said Maud. She didn't want to get that sickly theme tune stuck in her head.

"You should listen to it," said Milly. "You could learn from its message."

Milly stomped off to the bathroom and brushed her teeth while humming along loudly.

Maud felt a tingle in her toes. It spread up her legs, filling them with pins and needles. Then the toe of her left foot started to swing back and forth. She tried to stop it, but she couldn't control it. Her right foot began to move, too.

Maud gasped. Both her feet were tapping to the 'Pink Princess Pony Party Friendship Song'.

Her feet stepped from side to side with the rhythm. Maud glanced at herself in the mirror. For the first time in her life, she was dancing in time. But why was it happening now, when she wasn't even trying?

Milly came back in and looked at Maud.

"So you're dancing now?" asked Milly. "But dancing's my thing."

"I don't know how I'm doing it," said Maud. "And I don't know how to stop!"

Maud felt her feet twist. The top half of her body spun around, and she found herself sticking her arms out.

"There's no need to show off," snapped Milly.

"I'm sorry," said Maud. "This has never happened before."

Maud's legs spread into the splits, and she plunged down to the ground as the track came to an end.

"Yeah, right," said Milly, storming out of the room.

Maud scrambled up. She seemed to have control over her legs again, so she dashed downstairs, wondering if her dancing had something to do with the spell. Was there such a thing as a dancing spell? Why on earth would a witch or wizard want to dance, anyway? They preferred spooky, moonlit forests to strobe-lit discos.

Maud opened the door and ran out. She desperately hoped her legs wouldn't start dancing again when she got to school. She didn't think she could cope with the embarrassment of breaking into a twirl in front of everyone.

Chapter Nine

As Maud clambered to the back of the school bus, she couldn't shake the song from her head. She even found herself humming it as she took the seat beside Wilf. The vehicle lurched away, and she stumbled forward. Wilf held out a hand to steady her.

"Thanks," she said.

"That's okay," said Wilf. "What's that awful song you were humming?"

"It's nothing," said Maud.

The bus turned off the main road on to the bumpy track to Rotwood. Maud was staring out into the gloomy forest beside it when she got an unbearable itch on her neck. She screwed her face up and scratched it. "Ow!"

"What's the matter?" asked Wilf. "You look like Warren when he's forgotten to put on his flea powder."

"I don't know," said Maud. The itch spread to her arms, and she scratched until her skin went red. Then it was in her hands. She noticed a small patch of fine hairs in the centre of her palm. She pulled at them, but they were rooted deep under her skin.

"Look," she whispered to Wilf, pointing at the hairs.

"How strange," he said. "I didn't know Tutus got that, too."

"We don't, usually," said Maud.

The bus pulled into the clearing of the forest, and Rotwood loomed up ahead. Maud itched her hand again, and pain shot through it. Her nails were really sharp.

Maud stared at her arms in confusion. There was soft, downy hair on them now. What was going on? She gritted her teeth and plucked a hair out. A thicker, darker one grew back in its place.

Maud's mind raced. It must have been the spell. Was she finally becoming some sort of monster?

She grabbed her waterproof coat from her rucksack and pulled it on. Whatever was happening to her, she didn't want the whole school gawping.

She clambered down from the bus and pulled up the hood of her coat.

"What's wrong?" asked Wilf.

"It's the hairs," said Maud. "I think they're something to do with a spell I tried this morning."

"That sounds very useful," said Wilf. "My uncle Walter suffers from terrible moulting in the summer. He'd love to know about the spell."

As Wilf stood up, Maud saw he'd left a few hairs on the bus seat.

"It looks like you're moulting, too," she said.

"Huh. That's weird," said Wilf.

They got off the bus and climbed up the steps to the school. In the dim light of the entrance hall, Maud could see the school caretaker, Mr Quasimodo, pouring a slimy green detergent on to the floor. He glared at her as she passed, letting the entire contents of the bottle spill.

"You forget shave this morning?" he said.

Maud lifted her hand up to her chin and felt a row of small, wiry hairs. Her cheeks flushed hotter as she walked up the spiral stairs to her class. Whatever these weird changes were, she wanted them to stop. The last thing she wanted was for Penelope to notice her wild new look.

Maud slunk over to her seat and stared down

at her desk while Mr Von Bat called the register.

"Montague?" he asked.

Maud tried to answer, but found herself letting out a short, high yowl instead. Laughter filled the room, but she kept her eyes fixed on her desk. Every time she blinked, thick eyebrow hairs dangled into her field of vision.

Mr Von Bat stamped towards her.

"I'm glad you enjoyed your little joke," he said, "because it's just earned you a deten ..."

He trailed off as Maud looked up at him.

"Dear me," he said. "You're looking a little ... unkempt. I think you ought to go to the school nurse."

Maud heard Penelope giggling on the other side of the class. "I think Wilf should go, too, Sir," she said. "He's made a mess under his chair."

Maud turned to look at Wilf. He was moulting so badly that patches of pale skin were visible on his cheeks. The floor around his desk looked like a hairdresser's at closing time.

"Yes, I think that's a good idea," said Mr Von Bat.

Wilf coughed a huge hairball on to his desk and rushed out of the room. Maud followed, clutching her face in her hairy palms.

"I've never shed like this before," said Wilf sadly, pulling a clump of hairs from his arm. "Sometimes I lose a bit of fur in the spring, but it's not supposed to all go at once."

Maud ran her tongue along the edge of her teeth. They'd thinned into sharp points.

"It's strange," said Maud. "It's as though I'm turning into a wolf and you're turning into a hu … and you're turning into a Tutu."

"I hope not," said Wilf. "No offence to Tutus, but Dad already thinks I don't act like a proper wolf."

Maud knocked on a wooden door with 'sick room' scrawled across it. The school nurse, a huge ogre with scaly, green skin and an apron covered in deep-red stains, beckoned them in.

"We're both unwell," said Maud. "Wilf's losing hair, and I'm gaining it."

The nurse grunted and pointed to a couple of battered wooden chairs at the side of the room.

She grabbed a cracked magnifying glass and peered at Wilf. She yanked a fistful of hair from the back of his head, sniffed it and tasted it. She waddled over to a cupboard at the far end of the room and came back with a large white tub. The label on the front read 'Just For Werewolves' and had a picture of a grinning middle-aged wolf.

The nurse dipped her fat fingers into the tub and rubbed the white cream on Wilf's face and arms. Thick hairs sprouted from his pores at once.

"Monstrous!" said Wilf, standing up. "Hope you get cured, too, Maud!"

Wilf ran out, and the nurse picked up the magnifying glass. Maud could see every bloodshot vein in her yellow eyes.

"You not well," she said. She handed Maud an old, black phone with a dial. "Call parents."

Maud stuck a long nail in the dial and dragged it round. Eventually, she got through to her dad's mobile.

"Maurice Montague speaking," he said.

"Hi, Dad," said Maud. "I'm not feeling well."

"Oh dear," he said. "What's the matter, sweetie?"

"I'm ... it's quite hard to explain," said Maud. "Can you come and pick me up?"

Maud heard a clank. "Not a good time," said her dad. "I'm right in the middle of fixing an engine. Do you think you could jump in a cab?"

"Not really," said Maud. She remembered the time Mr Quasimodo had tried to order a cab. As soon as he stooped down and grabbed the door handle, the driver had revved away, leaving the confused caretaker holding the detached door. Since then, Rotwood had been on the cab company's list of banned addresses.

"Alright, petal," said Mr Montague. "I'll get there as soon as I can."

Maud handed the phone back and went out into the corridor. She plodded downstairs, made her way through the entrance hall, and sat on the wide stone steps outside.

She sniffed the air. The dinner ladies were making slime soup again. That was the third time this week.

Maud sniffed again. She could also smell maggot pie and spider stew. But the kitchens were in a crypt below the school. Usually, it was only Wilf who could smell things so far away.

She stared into the gloomy forest that surrounded the school, and spotted a small grey squirrel leaping down on to the soggy leaves on the ground. Maud had to stop herself getting down on all fours and chasing it.

She fixed her eyes on the ground while she waited for her dad. It seemed like the best way to make sure she didn't do anything embarrassing.

Soon she could smell the tang of exhaust fumes and turned to see her dad's car pulling into the clearing.

Mr Montague got out and walked over to Maud, his face screwed up in confusion.

"Dear me," he said. "You don't look well at all."

He helped Maud to her feet and led her to the car.

Maud fixed her seatbelt, as her dad released the handbrake and turned his key in the ignition.

"Sorry about these potholes," he said, as they trundled down the bumpy road. "They can't be helping with your illness."

"Never mind that," said Maud. "Imagine what they're doing to your suspension."

Mr Montague looked at her in confusion. "You really aren't feeling yourself at all, are you?"

Maud had no idea why she'd mentioned suspension. She'd said it without thinking at all.

She wound the window down and stuck her

hand out. The breeze felt good against her skin.

Maud pulled her hand back in and saw that the thick hairs had blown away, leaving it completely smooth again. She stuck her other hand out of the window and watched as the breeze sheared the hairs away like a fine razor.

She stuck her head out and immediately felt cooler and lighter. She looked at her reflection in the wing mirror. Her face was completely smooth again. The itches were gone, too.

Maud wondered what she could have done to take the spell away. Whatever it was, she was glad. At least Milly hadn't seen her in hairy form. She'd have reached straight for her camera.

Mr Montague turned into the main road, and something inside the car squealed.

"Sounds like you've got a dodgy fan belt," said Maud.

"What's a fan belt?" asked Mr Montague.

"I don't know," said Maud. "The words just sort of popped into my brain. You must know, though."

Mr Montague screwed his face up. "I should know, shouldn't I? But it's sort of slipped my mind."

Maud examined her hands. Her sharp claws had shrunk into neat fingernails again.

Mr Montague changed lanes, and the car squealed again.

In her head, Maud had a clear image of a strap of rubber inside the car engine that was slightly out of place. She somehow knew that if she could straighten it out, the noise would stop.

"I'll take a look at it, if you like," she said.

"You can fix a fan belt just by looking at it?" asked Mr Montague.

"No, I mean I'll get the bonnet up and have a tinker," said Maud.

"Best not," said Mr Montague. "It'll be safer to get an expert to look at it."

Maud had never heard her dad turn down the chance to fix a car before. What on earth was going on?

A blue car with a curved bonnet drove past, and Maud turned to watch it.

"You don't see many of those," she said.

"What?" asked Mr Montague. "Blue cars?"

"No," said Maud. "Tatra 77s. Czech cars made in the 1930s."

Mr Montague pulled into their driveway, and Maud got out, leaving massive clumps of hair behind her.

As she passed the bonnet, Maud found herself reaching underneath, squeezing a latch and lifting it up.

"What on earth are you doing?" asked her dad.

"Just checking the oil," said Maud. She stopped and thought about it. "Actually, I don't know. I think I'd better go and lie down."

Maud went upstairs and lay down on her bunk. Images of car engines and exhaust systems filled her head, but she forced them out and thought about all the bizarre things that had happened to her that day. First she found she could dance. Then she turned as hairy as something from a zoo. Now she'd become an expert on cars. It was as if she'd picked up the talents of Milly, Wilf and her dad, one after the other.

Maud took the spell out of her pocket and stared at it again.

Brothers and sisters, skulls and bones,
Others' power for your own,
Touch or brush, steal or pinch,
Clutch or tap, it's a cinch.

Of course! she thought. It was a power-stealing spell. She'd touched her sister, Wilf and her dad one after the other, and taken their powers.

Maud closed her eyes and listened to a 2.0-litre turbocharged four-cylinder BMW engine driving past. She certainly knew a lot about cars now, but she didn't see how it was going to impress a hall full of monsters. The contest was just a day away now, and she was no closer to working out what to do.

Chapter Ten

Maud opened her eyes. Bright sunlight was streaming in underneath her bedroom curtains. She'd been woken up by a squealing that she'd assumed was her alarm but turned out to be Milly playing her clarinet solo.

Maud hauled herself out of bed. She'd slept all night with her clothes on. The car knowledge she'd taken from her dad must have bored her to sleep.

Milly rushed into their room and held out her clarinet. The metal parts had been bent back into shape.

"Hasn't the mender done a super duper job?" asked Milly. "And all in time for your school talent contest tonight."

"Yeah," said Maud, forcing a smile. "Brilliant." She had been hoping Milly had forgotten about that.

Milly pranced out into the hallway as Maud rooted through the piles of clothes on her floor for her lucky skull-and-crossbones t-shirt. It didn't seem to be there. And with the contest nearly upon her, she needed all the luck she could get.

She ran downstairs and grabbed Quentin from his cage, using a handkerchief so as not to touch him. She rushed out just in time to catch up with the rickety Rotwood bus.

The driver pulled away too fast as usual, but this time Maud made sure she didn't stumble into anyone. The last thing she wanted was to accidentally touch Zombie Zak and find her limbs falling off.

She stepped carefully down the aisle and sat down next to Wilf.

"Hi, Maud," he said. Thick fur was now covering his arms and cheeks again. "That cream worked a treat. They could enter me into the Werewolf of the Year Show with this pelt. You're looking better, too."

"Mustn't grumble," said Maud, shoving her hand up the bridge of her nose as if she were adjusting a pair of glasses. She looked out of the back window, where a black plume of smoke was obscuring the view. "What about this old banger, eh? Can you believe it passed its M.O.T.?"

"What's an M.O.T.?" asked Wilf.

"It stands for Ministry of ..." began Maud. "Actually, it's not important." She looked down at her lap. She needed to forget about cars and think about the contest. Surely there was still time to come up with a plan. She had all day, after all.

The bell tolled three times for the end of the day. Everyone stood up and cheered. Everyone except Maud.

She slumped over her desk. She'd spent all day desperately trying to come up with an idea for the contest, but she hadn't thought of anything. Now she'd be humiliated in front of everyone.

"I'd like to thank you all for your concentration," said Mr Von Bat. "But I can't because you spent the whole lesson staring at your watches and counting the minutes to your precious contest. Well, it's time now. Off you go."

He swished his cape and flounced out.

Maud gathered her pens into her case, as the other pupils surged out of the classroom.

Quentin stuck his clamped snout over the top of Maud's jacket pocket.

So this is it, thought Maud. *The show's here, and I still don't have a clue what I'm going to do.*

"Are you alright?" came a voice from the back of the room.

Maud looked around but she couldn't see anyone. She heard dainty footsteps clacking towards her.

"Oh, hi, Isabel," she said. "I'm just a little worried about the show. I don't have a talent, and now everyone's going to find out."

The chair next to Maud pulled away from the desk.

"I'm sure you'll be fine," said Isabel. "Everyone gets a little nervous at times like this."

Maud felt a hand touch hers.

Thick curls of golden hair unfurled in the air in front of Maud. Large blue eyes, a freckly nose and a smiling mouth gradually appeared.

A young girl was now sitting in front of Maud. Her smile dropped, and she looked around the room in confusion.

"Where have you gone?" asked the girl. "Is this your act?"

"Isabel?" asked Maud. "Is that you?"

Isabel peered forward. "So Tutus can go invisible, too? Why didn't you tell me?"

"Invisible?" spluttered Maud. She flipped over her pencil case to look at her reflection in the metal base. All she could see was the wall behind her. She really was invisible! She wondered if she could use this new power in the talent show. But she couldn't see how. It was hard to entertain people who couldn't see you.

Isabel gasped. She was gazing down at her arms and wiggling her fingers.

"I'm … I'm … visible," she said.

Maud lifted the bottom of her pencil case up to Isabel.

"Ooh," she said, prodding her cheeks and

patting her hair. "So that's what I look like."

"Sorry," said Maud. "I think that was my fault."

"Don't apologise," said Isabel. "No one in my family has ever been visible before. It makes our photo albums pretty dull."

Maud could hear a pipe-organ playing in the depths of the school.

"It's show time!" said Isabel. She climbed up on the desk and leapt backwards, flipping over and landing gracefully on her feet with her arms outstretched. "Wish me luck."

"I don't think you'll need it," said Maud. "That was monstrous!"

"Thanks," said Isabel. She rushed out of the room. Maud dragged her pencil case into her bag and followed.

As she stepped along the hallway, she could hear loud applause coming from two floors below. In the glass of a display board, she saw the reflection of the wall behind her. It was as if she didn't exist. This was a disaster. If no one could see her, it was going to look like she'd chickened out of turning up at the talent show at all.

Chapter Eleven

A large wooden stage had been built at the back of the assembly hall. It had a small set of steps leading up to it. A banner was hanging down from the ceiling with "Rotwood's Got Talent" scrawled on it in red paint.

The pupils were watching from rows of wooden pews, while Maud paced around behind them, worrying about what she was going to do. She looked up at the stage, hoping desperately that she wasn't on next. Mr Quasimodo was dragging a series of hoops and jumps on to the stage. It looked like it was Wilf's turn.

The Head floated up on to the stage. Instead of her usual cardigan, she was wearing a smart black dress and a sparkly necklace. She looked up from her clipboard and shoved her large round glasses up her nose.

"Hello Rotwood!" shouted the Head. "Are you enjoying it so far?"

The crowd cheered and clapped their hands, paws and claws.

"Then without further ado," said the Head, "I'd like to welcome our next act to the stage ... Wilf Wild!"

The music teacher, Mr Fortissimo, began to play "Who Let the Dogs Out?" on his dusty pipe-organ, and Wilf padded up the steps. He got down on all fours and bounded around the stage. He ran across a see-saw, jumped over a wooden pole, slalomed between posts and jumped through a hoop. He came to a stop at the far end of the stage, got to his feet again and howled at the audience.

The crowd roared and screamed.

"Boring," shouted Penelope. She was sitting on the end of the back row next to Oscar. She had a feather boa draped over her shoulders and she'd sewn a few silver sequins to her black hat.

Maud stepped over and stood next to her, unseen.

"When is Maud on?" asked Penelope, smirking to herself. "She's the one I'm really looking forward to."

Oscar detached his head and held it above the crowd. "I don't think she's even here."

"She's probably too scared," said Penelope, "the talentless Tutu!"

Maud felt her cheeks heating up. She only just resisted the urge to knock Penelope's slightly-sparkly hat off.

Wilf bowed and stepped down from the stage, and the Head floated up again.

"What a fantastic act," she said. "Next up, it's the Vampire Flying Squad."

A colony of five bats swooped up on to the stage and flew around in a circle. They rose higher and higher in the air, spiralling around in perfect time. Or almost perfect time. The smallest one was slightly off the pace. Maud recognised it as Paprika.

Paprika almost crashed into the bat next to him, missing by just a couple of centimetres. Maud could barely watch. She tried covering her eyes with her hands, but it didn't work now she was invisible.

The bats hovered in a line above the stage. One by one, they looped twice in the air, transformed into human form in a puff of smoke, and landed gracefully on the stage. Paprika was on the end of the row. Maud winced. He'd always found transformation and landing difficult. If he got this wrong, he'd let the whole team down.

All the other vampires performed the move perfectly. Now it was Paprika's turn.

He plummeted down and looped around.

He looped again. And again. A tiny cloud of smoke appeared, and a full-sized Paprika spun out and landed on his feet. The crowd cheered loudly, and the vampires bowed.

"A triple loop!" said Oscar. "That was pretty monstrous."

"It was okay," scoffed Penelope. "But if you thought that puny display was impressive, wait until you see my spell show."

The Head glanced down at her piece of paper. "Next up, we've got ..."

Isabel stepped on to the stage. She was now wearing a blue leotard and pink leggings.

"Who are you?" asked the Head.

"I'm Visible Isabel, and this is my acrobatic display."

"Er ... right," said the Head, flipping through her notes. "Off you go."

The Head stepped down. Isabel launched herself into a cartwheel and landed gracefully on her feet. She held her hands out, and the audience clapped.

She sprung into a handstand, and everyone cheered.

"I'm up next," said Penelope. She bolted up and crashed right into Maud, glancing around with a confused frown before making her way down the aisle.

On the stage, Isabel vanished in the middle of a backwards handspring. There was a murmur from the pews, as everyone craned around to see where she'd gone.

Maud held her hands up and watched them slowly fade back into view from the fingernails down. She was becoming visible again. Maybe the spell was wearing off.

A few more footfalls sounded from the stage, and Isabel shouted, "Ta-dah!"

There was a thin smattering of applause from

the crowd, and the Head floated up again.

"Well, what did you think?" asked Isabel.

"It started well," said the Head. "But after that you lacked presence."

"Oh, not again," shouted Isabel. The sound of her feet stomping off the stage echoed around the hall.

Maud looked back down at her hands. In the flickering light of the hall, she saw that her skin had a green tinge.

Oh no! The spell wasn't wearing off at all. She'd touched Poisonous Penelope!

Chapter Twelve

Penelope was waiting at the side of the stage. Her skin was fading to pink now. She looked almost human.

The Head scanned her clipboard and looked up at the audience through her round glasses. "Let's hear it for Penelope Prenderghast."

Penelope grinned at the crowd as she climbed the steps. The green tone had completely gone from her skin, and her warts had shrunk to cute little freckles.

Maud raced down the aisle. "Stop!" she hissed. "Don't go on! I need to talk to you."

"Nice try," sneered Penelope. "I might have known you'd try and ruin it."

Penelope stepped on to the stage and cleared her throat. "I'd like to thank all my warm-up acts. Now it's time to witness some real talent. But a word of warning – if you see anyone fainting with amazement, please report them to the school nurse. Right, on with the show."

Penelope held her hands up to the audience, waggled her fingertips and shouted, "Abracadabra!"

Nothing happened.

Penelope glared at her hands. "I said, 'Abracadabra'!"

She tried thrusting her hands forward. "Come on. Work, you stupid things."

A couple of boos rang out from the crowd.

Maud could see the witch beginning to blush. Penelope had never been a friend, but Maud couldn't help feeling sorry for her. *I must be able to help her somehow*, she thought.

The words to the telekinesis spell popped into Maud's head. Maybe she could make Penelope float above the stage. It was hardly original after the vampire display, but it was better than nothing.

Maud recited the words of the spell backwards, slowly, then clicked her fingers and pointed at Penelope.

Penelope rose up in the air. She looked down at the stage with her eyes widening, and batted her arms and legs about.

Maud circled her hand around slowly, trying to make Penelope loop in the air like Paprika had done. Penelope's legs rose up over her head and came to a stop. Her black dress fell down over her head, exposing huge white bloomers to the crowd.

Giggles swept through the hall.

Maud spun her hand round quickly. Penelope turned in the air, her face now deep red. She whirled around faster and faster, her head and feet circling as if they were tied to a giant wheel.

Maud held her hand still, but Penelope only sped up, until she was a blur in the middle of the stage. A high screech echoed through the room. Not knowing what else to do, Maud clicked her fingers.

Penelope thumped down to the wooden stage, denting her black hat. She got to her feet and staggered towards the steps, her knees sagging. She tripped on the first step, and clattered down the rest to the floor.

There were a few nervous titters from the crowd.

Maud helped Penelope to her feet.

"Sorry," said Maud. "I tried to warn you."

"What? What happened?" asked Penelope.

"You had a bit of a funny turn," said Maud. "But I think you'll be alright now."

Penelope staggered off down the aisle, the green colour returning to her skin.

Maud was glad she'd given Penelope's powers back, but where did that leave her? She'd proved she had a talent for messing things up, but it was hardly one she could show off on stage.

The Head floated back up.

"Sorry about that, everyone," she said. "But I think we're ready to go on with the show again. Next up it's …"

The Head peered at her clipboard. "… Maud Montague."

Maud backed away down the aisle. There was no way she could go up on stage. All she had was a fire-breathing rat, and it would take more than that to entertain a hall full of genuine monsters.

Loud applause broke out. Maud looked up

at the stage. A girl who looked just like her was climbing the steps. She was even wearing her lucky skull-and-crossbones t-shirt.

"Uh-oh," muttered Maud.

It was Milly.

Chapter Thirteen

Maud's sister unfastened her case and lifted her clarinet out. It looked as though she'd gone through with her threat to turn up after all.

"I'm Maud Montague, and this is Mozart's Clarinet Concerto," she said.

She started to play.

All around the hall, pupils cried with pain and covered their ears.

"What the heaven is this?" shouted a demon in the row next to Maud. "It sounds almost … pretty."

Zombie Zak let out a low moan.

Milly reached the bit in the solo with the high notes and hit them perfectly. Maud had to admit, her sister was pretty good.

A loud groan went up. Oscar took his head off his shoulders and covered its ears.

"Someone stop her," shouted Professor Gool.

"Thisss is torture," hissed Dr Reaper, stretching his hood over his ears. "It'sss like something a human would enjoy."

Milly kept playing, oblivious to the distress she was inflicting. Maud ran down the aisle as the pupils and teachers around her began to yelp louder. She rushed on to the stage and tugged Milly's arm, just as she was building to her finale. The clarinet gave a squeaky honk like an angry goose.

A deep sigh of relief rose from the crowd.

Milly glared at Maud. "What did you do that for? I might have known you'd find a way to spoil my big moment."

"I can explain …" said Maud.

"I'm going to tell Mum and Dad," said Milly. She stomped down the steps and out of the hall.

Maud looked out across to everyone in the audience, who were watching her in silence. They all looked puzzled.

A few rows back, Wilf was staring at her with his hairy brow knotted. In all the time she'd known him, he'd never lied to her. And yet she'd never told him the truth about herself.

Paprika was sitting a couple of rows behind. She'd admitted to him that she was human, and he'd stayed friends with her. But would the other Rotwood monsters accept her as well? She didn't think so.

"What'sss going on?" asked Dr Reaper.

Maud heard the Head clear her throat at the side of the stage and turned to look at her. Her great-aunt Ethel just smiled and gave a nod. Mr Von Bat stood behind her. He mouthed, "Be yourself."

He was right. It had all gone on too long. Maud was sick of lying to everyone. It was time to come clean.

"I've got something to tell you all," said Maud. "That girl was my twin sister, Milly. She learned that clarinet piece for the talent contest at her school, Primrose Towers."

There were murmurs from the crowd.

"I know that I'm supposed to be sharing my monster skills with you right now, but I can't. The truth is that I don't have any monster skills, because I'm not a monster at all. I'm a human."

A loud gasp echoed around the ancient hall.

On the front row, Billy Bones' jaw dropped right off, and he had to stoop to pick it up.

Mr Galahad the games teacher rattled his armoured fist. "If you're a human, what the blazes are you doing at a school for monsters?"

"It was all a bit of a mix-up," said Maud. "When I first joined, I didn't even know Rotwood was a monster school. But I really loved it. So when you all asked me what sort of a monster I was, I invented one called a Tutu."

Maud forced a smile. "Sorry, everyone."

Dr Reaper stood up, pointing his pale, bony finger at Maud. "Impossster," he hissed.

Maud's heart sank. This was just what she'd been dreading. She'd spoiled the talent contest for everyone, and tomorrow she was almost certainly going to be expelled.

"I suppose you're right," she said. She was trying to speak clearly, but her voice came out cracked and uneven. "Until a couple of weeks ago, I was really enjoying myself here. But since this show was announced, I've had to admit that I don't have any monster talents. So maybe I don't belong here."

Maud glanced across the silent crowd, then turned towards the steps.

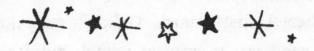

"You do belong," shouted a voice from a few rows back.

Maud peered into the crowd. Paprika had risen to his feet.

"It doesn't matter if you're human or not," he said. "You're a monster at heart. When I was worried about sports day, you taught me how to be fierce enough to win."

Wilf stood up, too. "Yeah, and that time we went camping, you helped me stand up to the Beast of Oddington."

On the front row, Billy Bones rose to his feet. "And you helped me with my venomous beasts homework that time. You know loads about spiders and stuff."

Oscar leapt up and shouted from the back. "You caught my head when it was about to land in some nettles. That was pretty monstrous."

Zombie Zak stood up. "Ug!"

Wilf started clapping, then Paprika and the Vampire Display Team joined in. Row by row, the monsters added to the applause. A group of demons flapped their wings in time at the back of the hall.

As Maud gazed out over the clapping pupils, her eyes filled with tears, blurring her view. She swallowed a lump in her throat.

"Sssssssilence," shouted Dr Reaper. "Thisss girl should not be here!"

Mr Galahad turned his head to look at the crowd. "Hear, hear. Maud might be popular, but allowing human pupils simply won't do. Whatever next? Human teachers?"

He snorted, and his moustache twitched up and down.

Mr Von Bat stepped forward. "Actually, you've already got one of those."

He strode across the stage, stripping off his cape and tossing it to the side.

"The truth is, I'm not a vampire at all. I'm a human, and my real name is Norman Bottom."

The crowd gasped even louder than before. Mr Von Bat reached into his mouth, pulled out his fake fangs and held them up. "I bought these from a joke shop, and frankly they've been getting on my nerves."

He tossed the plastic teeth over his shoulder and walked up to Maud, clasping her on the shoulder.

"And this is the girl who's given me the courage to confess," he said. "Just yesterday, I told her she needed to be herself. And yet I was living a lie. Well, there will be no more lies from now on."

On the front row, Billy Bones rose to his feet and chanted, "No more lies!"

One by one, the rest of the crowd stood up and joined in.

"I don't even like the taste of blood!" shouted Paprika.

"I've got fleas!" yelled Warren.

"I wear a wig!" grunted Mr Quasimodo, lifting up the tuft of hair on the top of his head to reveal a bald, green lump.

The Head rose a few feet above the stage and shouted, "That's quite enough!"

The noise cut out, and everyone sat back down.

"I need to discuss this with my colleagues," said the Head. "Staff, to the crypt!"

As the teachers filed from the hall, Mr Von Bat followed.

"Not you, Mr Bottom," said the Head.

Mr Von Bat blushed and hung his head in shame.

As the Head left the hall, Maud thought she saw her great-aunt give her a swift wink, but she couldn't be sure. Even if the Head wanted her to stay at Rotwood, the rest of the staff might not.

Maud slumped on the steps. This was it. They'd never let her stay. They couldn't change the rules just for her.

As the students muttered among themselves, Paprika and Wilf came over.

"You were great," said Paprika. "I don't feel so bad about having a human dad any more. Humans can be pretty monstrous sometimes."

"Thanks," said Maud.

"You could have told me you were human," said Wilf. "I wouldn't have minded."

"Sorry," said Maud. "I meant to. But it was hard to talk about."

A few minutes later, the Head led the teachers back into the hall. They all wore grim expressions, Dr Reaper's even grimmer than usual. Silence fell over the students.

"Now, Miss Montague," said the Head. "As

you know, this institution has rules."

Maud's shoulders sank. This didn't sound good.

"Humans are not allowed here," said the Head. "The reason for this is very simple. For centuries, your lot have persecuted us monsters. You've burnt us, walloped stakes through our hearts and drenched us with holy water. This school was meant to be a refuge from humans, not for humans."

Maud could see Dr Reaper's thin lips forming into a frown beneath the shadows of his cowl. Mr Galahad was shaking his head, his red cheeks wobbling. Professor Gool was staring down, his white tufts drooping.

"However," said the Head, "if we applied this rule to all humans, we'd be guilty of persecution, too. We have to accept that a human can be just as fierce and smart as a monster. And you, Maud Montague, are one such human."

Maud's heart was thumping in her chest.

"Does that mean I can stay?" she asked.

"You certainly can," said the Head.

Professor Gool and Mr Galahad applauded. Dr Reaper joined in, though he was gritting his long, thin teeth.

The other students all clapped as well.

All apart from Penelope.

Chapter Fourteen

Maud was woken by a blast of sound right in her ear. She sat up dizzily and rubbed her eyes. Milly was holding the end of her clarinet over Maud's ear. "Wakey-wakey," she said, and gave another toot for good measure.

The events of the previous night came flooding back.

"I said I'm sorry," said Maud, plugging her ears with her fingers. In fact, she'd said sorry about a thousand times. When she'd finally left Rotwood last night, Milly and their mum had been waiting for her in the car park. Milly had moaned about Maud ruining her performance all the way home.

"Well, it looks as though you haven't spoiled things as much as you wanted," said Milly, "because a teacher from your school called Professor Gool has invited me to play for his mother-in-law."

"That's nice," said Maud. She thought that Professor Gool must really hate his mother-in-law.

The doorbell rang, and Maud used the excuse to get out of the bedroom. When she opened the door, Penelope was standing there, one hand holding her broomstick and the other on her hip.

"Hi, Penelope," said Maud.

"You were using a power-stealing spell," said Penelope. "That's what happened yesterday, isn't it?"

"Yes," said Maud. "But it was all a mistake. One of the pages fell out of your spell book and

I read it out. I didn't even know what it did."

Penelope narrowed her eyes. "So you didn't steal my powers deliberately?"

"Of course not," said Maud. "It was you who touched me, anyway. I even tried to help you by casting the telekinesis spell. Sorry I messed it up."

"Messed it up?" squealed Penelope. "That's putting it mildly." Then, out of nowhere, a smile appeared on her face. "Come on, then. Don't you want me to take the spell off?"

"Really?" asked Maud. "This isn't a trick? You're not going to turn me into a frog or something?"

"It's tempting," said Penelope. "But no. I just think it will be safer for everyone this way. Quick, before I change my mind."

"Just give me a moment," said Maud. "There's something I have to do first. Follow me."

Maud dashed through to the garage, where Quentin was snoozing in his cage.

"He's not that monstrous," said Penelope, peering into the cage. "But he's sort of okay."

"Thanks," said Maud.

"You know," said Penelope, "I never really hated you."

"So why do you always act like you do?" asked Maud.

Penelope shrugged. "I guess I didn't like the idea that a Tutu could be more monstrous than me." She held out her hand. "Friends?"

Maud was about to shake, when she remembered the spell. "Better do the magic first," she said. "Hang on a sec."

Maud reached into Quentin's cage and touched him.

At once, she felt a heat in her throat and the urge to burp. She threw her head back, and released a jet of fire into the air. Penelope ducked with a yelp.

"Watch it, Montague!" she said.

Maud blinked through a heat haze. "Sorry. I

just wanted to take Quentin's power away. Plus, I couldn't resist finding out what it felt like. Okay, ready now."

Penelope muttered under her breath and wiggled her fingers.

"Done," she said.

Maud tried a fiery burp, but it was just a normal burp this time. "Thanks!" she said.

She took off Quentin's muzzle. He looked down at the end of his snout and squeaked nervously. No fire came out. He looked at Maud and gave a toothy grin.

"You know, as humans go, you're not that terrible," said Penelope.

"Thanks," said Maud. She thought it was the closest thing to a compliment she'd ever get from Penelope.

The witch tapped her broomstick on the ground. "Fancy a lift to school?"

"Monstrous," said Maud.

Twenty minutes later, Penelope touched

down by the front of the school, and Maud climbed off the broom. The Rotwood students were gathered around the notice board once again. Maud saw a new piece of parchment pinned up with a dagger.

ROTWOOD TALENT SHOW RESULTS

3rd place - Penelope Prenderghast for her slapstick comedy display

2nd place - Paprika Von Bat and the Vampire Flying Squad

1st place - Maud Montague for her impression skills. By successfully impersonating a monster all year, Maud Montague has proved beyond doubt that she's the most talented pupil at Rotwood.

The students crowded around her, clapping her on the back and muttering, "Well done, Montague!" and "Monstrous show!"

Maud stood in front of the board, savouring the moment. The other pupils wandered away, and at last, she was all alone, with Rotwood Forest whispering around her.

"Don't dawdle, Montague," said a voice she recognised.

Maud turned to see a man wearing a knitted tank-top and beige slacks with neatly parted hair. At first Maud wondered if it was one of her dad's friends. But as she approached him, she saw it was actually Mr Von Bat without his vampire costume.

"You look different," she said.

"It's a lot more comfortable than my usual stuff," said Mr Von Bat. "The amount of times

I've got that cape caught in the car door."

"So should I call you Norman from now on?" asked Maud.

"Don't be cheeky," said her teacher. "It's Mr Bottom to you."

Maud followed him up the steps into the school. It was just another ordinary day at Rotwood – and she couldn't stop smiling.

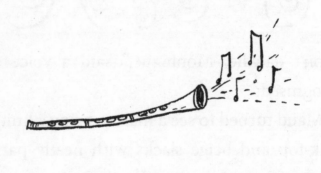

Other titles by A. B. Saddlewick:

ISBN: 978-1-78055-072-5

ISBN: 978-1-78055-073-2

ISBN: 978-1-78055-074-9

ISBN: 978-1-78055-075-6

ISBN: 978-1-78055-172-2